ISAAC ASIMOV'S NEW LIBRARY OF THE UNIVERSE

SCIENCE FICTION:
VISIONS OF TOMORROW?

BY ISAAC ASIMOV
WITH REVISIONS AND UPDATING BY GREG WALZ-CHOJNACKI

Gareth Stevens Publishing
MILWAUKEE

For a free color catalog describing Gareth Stevens' list of high-quality books, call 1-800-542-2595 (USA) or 1-800-461-9120 (Canada). Gareth Stevens' Fax: (414) 225-0377.

Library of Congress Cataloging-in-Publication Data

Asimov, Isaac.
  Science fiction: visions of tomorrow? / by Isaac Asimov; with
revisions and updating by Greg Walz-Chojnacki.
    p. cm. — (Isaac Asimov's New library of the universe)
  Rev. ed. of: Science fiction, science fact. 1989.
  Includes index.
  ISBN 0-8368-1224-7
  1. Science—Juvenile literature. 2. Science fiction—Juvenile
literature. [1. Science fiction—History and criticism.
2. Forecasting.] I. Walz-Chojnacki, Greg, 1954-.
II. Asimov, Isaac. Science fiction, science fact. III. Title.
IV. Series: Asimov, Isaac. New library of the universe.
Q163.A86   1995
500—dc20   95-7233

This edition first published in 1995 by
Gareth Stevens Publishing
1555 North RiverCenter Drive, Suite 201
Milwaukee, Wisconsin 53212, USA

Series editor: Barbara J. Behm
Design adaptation: Helene Feider
Production director: Teresa Mahsem
Editorial assistant: Diane Laska
Picture research: Mathew Groshek and Diane Laska

Printed in the United States of America

1 2 3 4 5 6 7 8 9 99 98 97 96 95

To bring this classic of young people's information up to date, the editors at Gareth
Stevens Publishing have selected two noted science authors, Greg Walz-Chojnacki
and Francis Reddy. Walz-Chojnacki and Reddy coauthored the recent book *Celestial
Delights: The Best Astronomical Events Through 2001*.

Walz-Chojnacki is also the author of the book *Comet: The Story Behind Halley's
Comet* and various articles about the space program. He was an editor of *Odyssey*, an
astronomy and space technology magazine for young people, for eleven years.

Reddy is the author of nine books, including *Halley's Comet, Children's Atlas of the
Universe, Children's Atlas of Earth Through Time*, and *Children's Atlas of Native
Americans*, plus numerous articles. He was an editor of *Astronomy* magazine for
several years.

CONTENTS

We live in an enormously large place – the Universe. It's just in the last fifty-five years or so that we've found out how large it probably is. It's only natural that we would want to understand the place in which we live, so scientists have developed instruments – such as radio telescopes, satellites, probes, and many more – that have told us far more about the Universe than could possibly be imagined.

We have seen planets up close. We have learned about quasars and pulsars, black holes, and supernovas. We have gathered amazing data about how the Universe may have come into being and how it may end. Nothing could be more astonishing.

Still, long before any of these discoveries were made, science fiction writers imagined what the future in space might hold. It was very difficult for these writers, despite their creativity, to guess just how incredible the Universe is. Still, they sometimes made remarkably good guesses. Let's compare science fiction with science fact.

Isaac Asimov

In the first science fiction movie ever made – *A Trip to the Moon* – a giant cannon on Earth *(right)* fires a bulletlike ship right into the "eye" of the Moon *(above).* The movie was made in 1902.

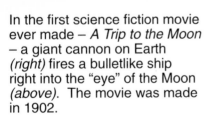

Early Science Fiction

For centuries – even in ancient Roman times – writers have imagined travel to the Moon. With the coming of the Industrial Revolution in the 1800s, writers could imagine even more. They could see how machines were changing the world. For example, a French science fiction writer, Jules Verne, wrote about submarines and about a spaceship shot to the Moon by a cannon fired from Florida!

An English science fiction writer, H. G. Wells, wrote a story in 1908 called "The War in the Air." The story described the bombing of cities from the air. Wells wrote about atomic bombs in "The World Set Free" in 1914. In his 1901 story, "The First Men in the Moon," Wells wrote about people floating to the Moon in a ship that defied gravity.

? *The first science fiction story?*

How old is science fiction? Some people think Homer's Odyssey *is science fiction; others say it is only fantasy. Some say you can't have science fiction unless you base it on new developments in science. Some think* Frankenstein *is the first science fiction story; others say it's only gothic romance. Some say you need solid science in your story and that "Five Weeks in a Balloon" is the first science fiction story. This dispute will probably never be settled.*

A Journey to Worlds Beyond

Amazing Stories, the first magazine devoted entirely to science fiction, began publication in 1926. Contributors to the magazine often wrote about rockets that traveled to the Moon and to other planets and their moons.

In 1928, one exciting story, "The Skylark of Space," described voyages to the stars. Sometimes the magazine would describe other planets as being inhabited by hostile aliens. Martians were often treated as being a dangerous threat to Earth.

❗ *Life imitating art*

In 1941, Robert A. Heinlein wrote a story describing the invention of the atomic bomb. This later came true. Isaac Asimov wrote about robots forty years before they were a reality. He was the first person to use the word robotics, *now in common use. He also described the pocket computer in 1950, twenty years before it came into use.*

Top: Flying saucers are not a recent phenomenon – just look at this magazine cover from 1918!

Bottom: Early publications throughout the world contained science fiction articles. This magazine containing "sci-fi" stories was published in France in 1908.

Opposite: Humans meet aliens on the cover of this 1927 magazine.

Robots: Machines Working for Humans

Early in this century, science fiction writers wrote about robots – machines that could take the place of the work done by humans. Some thought robots would be common in homes by the end of the twentieth century. Today, the reality of robots is slightly different. Robots don't yet do our housework, but they are a growing part of life.

The spacecraft that visit worlds far away are simple robots. More complex and intelligent machines are being built each day. These robots can safely wander over alien terrain that is too dangerous and expensive for humans to explore. Robots can also explore dangerous places on Earth – such as volcanoes.

Left: This rover, a type of robot, will be able to explore the surface of Mars with little instruction from Earth.

Opposite: This robot, called Dante, has visited the inside of a volcano on Earth. Entering volcanoes is an important way to learn about them. Unfortunately, it is a risky job for humans that has, in the past, claimed the lives of many scientists.

A Long, Slow Process

Most science fiction writers in history have described rocket ships as quickly crossing the Solar System as though they were airplanes easily jetting from New York to Los Angeles. In reality, it would take rockets months to travel to Mars and years to reach the distant outer planets.

If rockets kept their engines firing, they could go a little faster. But rockets simply cannot carry enough fuel to do that for long.

Below: In 1638, a story called "The Man in the Moon" by Francis Godwin was published. In the story, geese fly a man to the Moon.

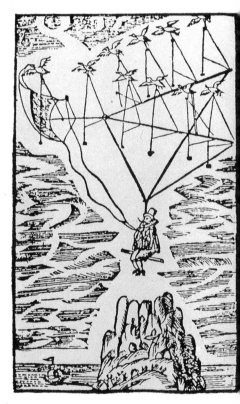

! *Rockets win the space race*

Rockets are the only way so far to launch humans and equipment into space. The English scientist Sir Isaac Newton first explained the law by which rockets work. But the first person to actually suggest rockets for use in space travel was writer Cyrano de Bergerac. He mentioned rockets in his 1656 novel about a Moon voyage. He also mentioned six other ways to reach the Moon – none of which would have worked.

Opposite: A modern computer game *(inset)* is used to test psychokinesis. This is the process by which the human mind alone is able to move physical objects. This as-yet-unproven ability may one day power spaceships to the remote reaches of space.

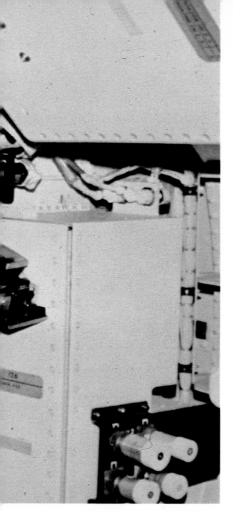

Zero Gravity

In early science fiction stories, space travelers did not appear to be experiencing zero gravity, or weightlessness. Probably early writers assumed there would be some sort of artificial gravity on board spaceships.

In reality, space travelers must overcome the difficulties of weightlessness. One cosmonaut lived almost two-thirds of a year with the challenges presented by the weightlessness of space.

Opposite: Cosmonauts aboard Russian space station *Mir (top)* and astronauts aboard U.S. space station *Skylab (bottom)* have had to deal with weightlessness and cramped living conditions.

Left, top and bottom: In the original *Star Trek*, occupants of the fictional *U.S.S. Enterprise*, a twenty-third-century starship, lived with the sensation of gravity and in spacious quarters.

The Moon of Fact and Fiction

Science fiction writers want their stories to be exciting. But making a story exciting doesn't always make it accurate.

Jules Verne described a trip to the Moon but didn't have his characters land on the Moon. H. G. Wells's stories had people landing on the Moon. For more excitement, they encountered an advanced civilization.

But the Moon in fact has not been like the Moon in fiction. When humans actually did land on the Moon in 1969, they found no civilization. The Moon was a completely lifeless world.

When the first Moon landing with humans on board was made, hundreds of millions of people on Earth watched it on television. That was one scientific achievement the early science fiction writers hadn't thought of – watching the first Moon landing on television!

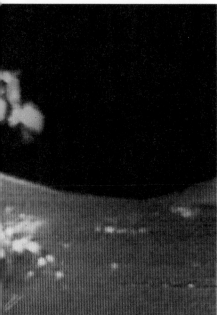

Top: Pictured is a scene from *The First Men in the Moon*, a 1964 movie based on a story by H. G. Wells. In the story line, United Nations astronauts are surprised to find a British flag and other evidence of earlier Moon visitors.

Opposite, bottom left: U.S. Astronaut Edwin "Buzz" Aldrin poses near an American flag left on the Moon by the *Apollo* crew in 1969.

Bottom, right: In this television image, a camera remotely controlled from Houston made it possible for people on Earth to watch this spectacular lift-off from the Moon's surface in 1972.

Our Future in Space

In order for people to live in space, they will also have to work there. For this to become a reality, a space station will have to be built close to Earth. There, people could permanently live, work, and construct new spaceships for exploration farther out in space.

Large settlements like this do not yet exist. But humans are already working in space. Astronauts have repaired several satellites while in orbit, including the Hubble Space Telescope. Astronauts have also practiced putting pieces of a space station together. These pioneering efforts are the first steps toward creating human habitations in space.

Right: U.S. Astronaut Kathryn C. Thornton refers to instructions on her arm to assist her in repairing the Hubble Space Telescope while in orbit in 1993.

Opposite: In 1951, scientist Wernher von Braun and artist Chesley Bonestell predicted a piloted mission to Mars with a reusable space vehicle, a space station, and an orbiting telescope. Bonestell's drawing is at *top*. A more recent NASA illustration *(bottom)* features a space shuttle, space station, and observation satellite. This drawing shows that the von Braun/Bonestell prediction was right on target.

Terraforming Other Worlds

Early science fiction writers assumed that all the planets in our Solar System were fairly Earthlike. Some pictured settlers on Venus hunting dinosaurs. Some imagined grain fields on Mars, irrigated by water from canals. As scientists learned that the atmospheres on other planets were not breathable, writers invented domed or underground cities with Earthlike atmospheres.

Scientists want to change the atmosphere on Mars to make human habitation possible there. The process of making planets Earthlike is called terraforming. People could live on such a terraformed Mars without domed cities or space suits. Will this science fiction be fact in a few hundred years?

! Two satellites for Mars – moons before their time

In the book, Gulliver's Travels, *Jonathan Swift wrote about a fictional land where astronomy was very advanced. In that land, astronomers discovered that Mars had two small satellites. The book was written in 1726, when no such satellites were known. It was not until 150 years later that two satellites were actually discovered, orbiting Mars, similar to what Swift had described. Swift had made a guess based on the ideas of scientist Johannes Kepler.*

Right: In his 1726 book, *Gulliver's Travels*, author Jonathan Swift invented the floating island of Laputa.

Center: This scene could be from an imaginary visit to Venus or to prehistoric Earth.

Opposite: Pictured is an artist's view of a refinery of the future on a moon of Uranus called Umbriel.

What Lies Among the Stars?

Science fiction writers have imagined different forms of life on various planets. Quite often writers have depicted these fictional life-forms as being intelligent and perhaps even hostile to humans.

Sometimes, the writers of books, films, and television shows imagine that beings from different worlds join some sort of confederation or political union. This might be described as a galactic federation or a galactic empire.

In reality, there is no actual evidence – at least not yet – that any life exists beyond Earth. But still we dream of seeking – and finding – advanced life-forms among the stars.

Opposite: In this drawing, space probes descend from a giant ship to explore a strange new world.

Inset: As Earth civilization expands into space, Earthlings may run into other civilizations. Perhaps Earthlings will even be invited to join a galactic federation made up of different life-forms in the Milky Way.

21

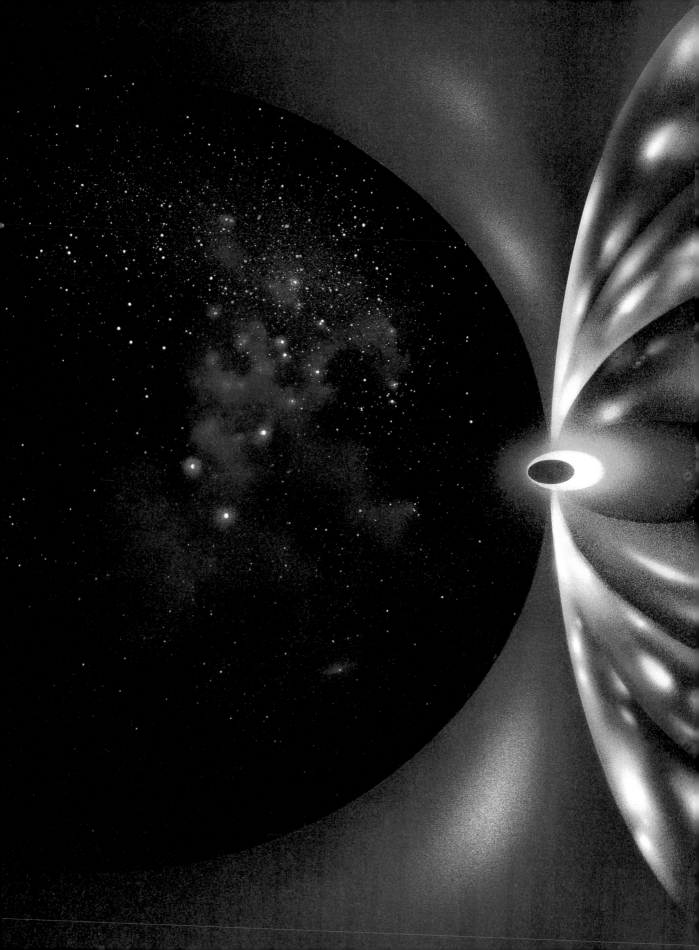

Faster Than the Speed of Light

The idea of star travel is appealing, but it presents great challenges. For instance, how would people travel from one star to the next? How would various settlements communicate with each another? Since 1905, scientists have known that nothing can travel faster than the speed of light – 186,000 miles (300,000 kilometers) a second. It is too fast a speed for humans to travel.

However, science fiction writers often take liberties and break the laws of nature. They imagine something like "hyperspace" through which spaceships can travel faster than the speed of light.

Left: An artist's conception of a starship traveling at nearly the speed of light.

Truth – More Incredible Than Fiction

Science fiction writers of the past had very creative imaginations, but they usually underestimated just how incredible future space technology would become.

In 1900, most writers who visualized air flight thought of advanced dirigibles and small airplanes. They imagined rocket ships going to the Moon, but they didn't think of all the myriad of ways in which space could be put to practical use. In early times, most writers did not think of communications satellites, weather satellites, or navigational satellites.

However, some early writers did think of space suits very much like those that have actually been used by the space program. They also imagined things like microfilm, tape recorders, lasers, and even charge cards. In many instances, science fiction writers of long ago were accurate in their predictions.

Above: A rocket belt whisks its comic-book hero away from the clutches of villains.

Below: In 1649, Cyrano de Bergerac wrote "Voyage to the Moon," the story of a man who straps bottles of morning dew to his waist and uses the power of evaporation to float upward.

Opposite: A rocket belt in its most modern form — the manned maneuvering unit (MMU) — is put through its first run outside the shuttle *Challenger* in 1984.

❗ *Science fiction's popularity on the rise*

For years, science fiction authors wrote their stories, but the works did not have a wide-ranging appeal. Then, in the 1980s, the popularity of science fiction blossomed. Computers, robots, and trips to the Moon apparently have put people in a science fiction type of mood. In addition, blockbuster movies have increased the public's appetite for science fiction.

A Peaceful Venture into Space

Science fiction writers have often envisioned war in space, but they have tended to picture air battles. They have imagined space ships maneuvering rapidly to shoot each other down with disintegrator rays. In today's reality, disintegrator rays are laser beams manipulated by computers.

Despite some of the differences between science fact and fiction, a real war in space could match or surpass fictional wars in one way – a real war holds the terrible power to actually destroy our planet. How devastating that would be! Certainly that is not why humans have ventured into space.

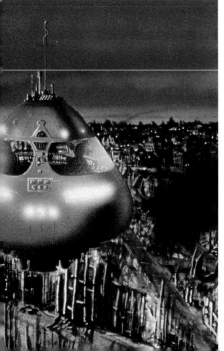

Top: Imperial stormtroopers, X-Wing fighters, and Darth Vader *(inset)* – all creations of the movie *Star Wars.* The movie tells the story of a galaxy-wide civil war.

Opposite, bottom left: So far, no war has ever been fought in space. But space weapons for the purpose of destroying satellites have been designed by both the United States and Russia.

Left: A war utilizing space vehicles as instruments of destruction could be devastating to our planet.

27

Fact File: First Fiction, Then Fact

Science fiction writers try to predict the future. But many things described in science fiction, such as travel to other galaxies and time travel, seem impossible. These ideas sound too far-fetched to ever become a reality.

But many topics that science fiction writers of long ago wrote about really do exist today – sometimes years, or even centuries, before even *they* thought their ideas would become a reality!

For instance, most people in the 1800s probably would have thought that inventions like cellular telephones, air-conditioned skyscrapers, and spacecraft were pure fantasy. But these – and many other inventions dreamed up by science fiction writers have become a big part of modern life. Sometimes, science fiction does become science fact!

Modern Inventions That Were Once the Dreams of Science Fiction Writers

Invention	Predicted By	Date Actually Invented
Air-conditioned skyscrapers	Jules Verne *In the Twenty-Ninth Century – The Day of an American Journalist* (1875)	1930
Artificial intelligence (including computers that can "think" for themselves)	Ammianus Marcellinus (Aaron Nadel) "The Thought Machine," *Amazing Stories* magazine (1927)	1950s-present
Atomic energy	H. G. Wells *The World Set Free* (1914)	1942
Charge cards	Edward Bellamy *Looking Backward, 2000-1887* (1888)	1952
Lasers	Sir Francis Bacon (1626)	1960
Long-distance submarines	Jules Verne *Twenty Thousand Leagues Under the Sea* (1870)	1950s-present
Microfilm	Hugo Gernsback *Ralph 124C 41+* (1911)	1920
Navigational satellites	Edward Everett Hale (1870)	1959
News broadcasts	Jules Verne, *In the Twenty-Ninth Century...* (1875)	1920
Robots	Karel Capek, *R. U. R. (Rossum's Universal Robots)* (1921)	1920s-present
Space suits	Frank R. Paul, *Amazing Stories* magazine (1939)	1950s and 1960s
Spacecraft that could carry people to the Moon	Jules Verne, *From the Earth to the Moon* (1865) H. G. Wells, *The First Men in the Moon* (1901)	1960s
Tape recorders	Hugo Gernsback *Ralph 124C 41+* (1911)	1936
Television	Jules Verne, *In the Twenty-Ninth Century...* (1875) H. G. Wells, *The Time Machine* (1895)	1920s
Test-tube babies	Aldous Huxley, *Brave New World* (1931)	1978

More Books about Science Fiction

Aliens and Extraterrestrials – Are We Alone? Asimov (Gareth Stevens)
Astronomy in Ancient Times. Asimov (Gareth Stevens)
The Donkey Planet. Corbett (Dutton)
The First Men in the Moon. Wells (Airmont)
I Was a Second Grade Werewolf. Pinkwater (Live Oak Media)
Meet E. T. the Extra-Terrestrial. Klimo (Simon and Schuster)
Star Trek: Voyage into Adventure. Dodge (Archway)
The War of the Worlds. Wells (Putnam)

Videos

Astronomy 101: A Beginner's Guide to the Night Sky. (Mazon)
Mars: Our Mysterious Neighbor. (Gareth Stevens)
There Goes a Spaceship. (KidVision)

Places to Visit

Most towns, especially larger cities and towns with colleges and universities, have libraries and bookstores that have collections of science fiction. Also, many cities have used and rare book bookshops, as well as new and used comic book bookshops. These shops often carry a wide selection of science fiction materials.

The Fantasy Foundation has one of the largest collections of science fiction literature and artwork, including posters and souvenirs of science fiction movies, in the world.

The Fantasy Foundation
Forrest J. Ackerman's Archive of the Fantastic
2495 Glendower Avenue
Hollywood, CA 90027

The Fantasy Foundation is open to the public most Saturdays, but telephone ahead at 213-666-6326.

Places to Write

Here are some places you can write for more information and answers to your questions about science fiction. Be sure to state what kind of information you would like. Include your full name and address so they can write back to you.

Los Angeles Science Fantasy Society
11513 Burbank Boulevard
North Hollywood, CA 91601

Baltimore Science Fiction Society, Inc.
P. O. Box 686
Baltimore, MD 21203

Glossary

aliens: in this book, beings from some place other than Earth.

artificial: imitation; manufactured by people instead of occurring in nature.

astronaut: an American who travels beyond Earth's atmosphere.

astronomy: the scientific study of the Universe and its various bodies.

atmosphere: the gases surrounding a planet, star, or moon.

atomic bomb: a bomb that gets its power from the energy released when atoms under great pressure fuse or divide. When this enormously destructive device explodes, its blast can kill all forms of life both right away and more slowly, through the release of radiation that causes illness.

black hole: an object in space created by the explosion and collapse of a star. This object is so tightly packed that not even light can escape the force of its gravity.

cosmonaut: a Russian who travels beyond Earth's atmosphere.

Cyrano de Bergerac: a French writer known for his plays and fantasies.

dirigible: an airship consisting of a balloon and a hold for the engine and passengers. The balloon is filled with hydrogen and helium gases to make it lighter than air.

disintegrator ray: an imaginary weapon that shoots a beam, breaking the target into fragments or turning it into vapor.

gothic romance: a story about a love affair that contains elements that are bizarre, mysterious, or ghostly.

Industrial Revolution: the change from a society that is based on agriculture into one based on manufacturing goods with machinery, on a large scale.

Kepler, Johannes: a German astronomer who lived from 1571 to 1630. He calculated a pattern of moons for the known planets of his day ranging from none for Venus, one for Earth, one or two for Mars, and four for Jupiter.

laser beam: a powerful ray of light that can be both precisely focused and intense enough to burn holes through the hardest materials known. Lasers are currently used for delicate surgery and for cutting gems.

NASA: the space agency in the United States – the National Aeronautics and Space Administration.

probe: a craft that travels in space, photographing celestial bodies and even landing on some of them.

pulsar: a star with all the mass of an ordinary large star but with that mass squeezed into a small ball. It sends out rapid pulses of light or electrical waves.

quasar: the starlike core of a galaxy that may have a large black hole at its center.

radio telescope: an instrument that uses a radio receiver and antenna both to see into space and to listen for messages from space.

robotics: the study and manufacture of robots, devices that can perform certain mechanical tasks.

satellite: a smaller body orbiting a larger body. Our Moon is Earth's natural satellite. Communication, weather, and navigational satellites are examples of artificial satellites of Earth.

Index

Born in 1920, Isaac Asimov came to the United States as a young boy from his native Russia. As a young man, he was a student of biochemistry. In time, he became one of the most productive writers the world has ever known. His books cover a spectrum of topics, including science, history, language theory, fantasy, and science fiction. His brilliant imagination gained him the respect and admiration of adults and children alike. Sadly, Isaac Asimov died shortly after the publication of the first edition of *Isaac Asimov's Library of the Universe*.

The publishers wish to thank the following for permission to reproduce copyright material: front cover, © Alan Gutierrez; 4, 4-5, The Museum of Modern Art Film Stills Archive; 6 (upper), Collection of Sam Moskowitz; 6 (lower), © National Library; 7, Collection of Sam Moskowitz; 8, Jet Propulsion Laboratory; 9, Courtesy of William Ingalls, NASA; 10, © Lee Bataglia; 11 (large), © Garret Moore; 11 (inset), © Institute for Parapsychology; 12, James Oberg Archive; 12-13 (upper), NASA; 12-13 (center and lower), Photofest; 14, NASA; 14-15 (upper), The Kobal Collection; 14-15 (lower), NASA; 16, Courtesy of Griffith Observatory; 16-17, © Sal Erato 1988; 17, © Alan Gutierrez; 18, NASA; 19 (upper), © Chesley Bonestell/Space Art International; 19 (lower), Courtesy of McDonnell Douglas; 20-21, © Alan Gutierrez; 21, © Julian Baum; 22-23, © Mark Paternostro 1988; 22 (upper), © David A. Hardy; 22 (lower), National Astronomy and Ionosphere Center/Cornell University; 23, © Mark Paternostro 1988; 24 (upper), Matthew Groshek/© Gareth Stevens, Inc.; 24 (lower), © Lee Bataglia; 25, NASA; 26 (upper), The Museum of Modern Art Film Stills Archive; 26 (lower), Courtesy of Los Alamos National Laboratory; 26-27 (upper), The Museum of Modern Art Film Stills Archive; 26-27 (lower), © Garret Moore; 28 (upper), © Steve Elmore/Tom Stack and Associates 1986; 28 (lower), The Museum of Modern Art Film Stills Archive; 29 (upper and center right), © Jon Feingersch/Tom Stack and Associates 1988; 29 (center left), © Claude Charlier/Science Source/Photo Researchers; 29 (lower right), Collection of Sam Moskowitz.